All profits from this book will be donated to charitable
organizations, with a gentle preference towards people
with my husband's disease – multiple sclerosis.

Vanita Oelschlager

Acknowledgements

Robin Hegan

Kristin Blackwood

Jennie Levy Smith

Mike Blanc

Kurt Landefeld

Paul Royer

Michael Olin-Hitt

Mother Goose, Other Goose
VanitaBooks, LLC
All rights reserved.
© 2008 VanitaBooks, LLC
No part of this book may be reproduced, stored in retrieval
systems, or transmitted in any form or through methods
including electronic photocopying, online download, or any
other system now known or hereafter invented – except by
reviewers, who may quote brief passages in a review to be
printed in a newspaper or print or online publication –
without express written permission from VanitaBooks, LLC.
Text by Vanita Oelschlager.
Illustrations by Robin Hegan.
Design by Trio Design & Marketing Communications Inc.
Printed in China.
ISBN 978-0-9800162-6-0

www.VanitaBooks.com

Mother Goose
Other Goose

written by Vanita Oelschlager *illustrated by* Robin Hegan

This book is dedicated to
all my grandchildren.
Vanita Oelschlager

To Matt, Kendall and Kya:
Thanks for supporting
Mommy's dreams!
Robin Hegan

Baa Baa Black Sheep

Baa, baa, black sheep,
Have you any wool?
Yes sir, yes sir,
Three bags full;

One for my master,
One for my dame,
And one for the little boy
That lives in our lane.

Little Baby Bare Feet

Little baby bare feet
Running in the grass.
Dingle dangle bare feet
In a pond with bass.

A bass for your mother,
A bass for your dad,
And none for your sister
Cause two's all you had.

Georgy Porgy

Georgy Porgy, pudding and pie,
Kissed the girls and made them cry.
When the boys came out to play,
Georgy Porgy ran away.

Marty Warty

Marty Warty
Told a lie.
He told it but
He didn't know why.
His father sent him
To his room.
He didn't get out
Till next day noon.

Mary, Mary, Quite Contrary

Mary, Mary quite contrary,
How does your garden grow?
Silver bells and cockle-shells,
And pretty maids all in a row.

Larry Harry Huckleberry

Larry Harry Huckleberry
On each foot had an extra toe.
It was a mess, but he did his best
To not let his feet ever show.

Jack and Jill

Jack and Jill went up the hill,
To fetch a pail of water;
Jack fell down, and broke his crown,
And Jill came tumbling after.

Jasper Snill

Jasper Snill lived on the hill,
His view was t'ward the water.
He never came down to visit the town,
Except to see his daughter.

Jack Sprat

Jack Sprat could eat no fat,
His wife could eat no lean;
And so, betwixt them both,
They licked the platter clean.

Ginny McVat

Ginny McVat was a little too fat.
She tried and she tried to slim down.
But all of her efforts failed it seems
She couldn't get into her gown.

Old Mother Hubbard

Old Mother Hubbard;
Went to the cupboard,
To give her poor dog a bone;
But when she got there,
The cupboard was bare,
And so the poor dog had none.

Floppy Eared Puppy

Floppy eared puppy
Was always hungry.
He went to his bowl for more food.
When he got there
The bowl was bare,
So floppy eared puppy boo-hooed.

It's Raining, It's Pouring

It's raining, it's pouring.
The old man is snoring.
He bumped his head,
And went to bed,
And didn't get up until morning.

He's Sleeping, He's Snoring

He's sleeping, he's snoring.
Outside it's pouring.
I'd go ahead,
And get out of bed,
But it's 2 o'clock in the morning.

Peter Piper

Peter Piper picked a peck of pickled peppers;
A peck of pickled peppers Peter Piper picked:
If Peter Piper picked a peck of pickled peppers,
Where's the peck of pickled peppers Peter Piper picked?

Biggy Piggy

Biggy Piggy boxed a box of bunny chocolates;
A box of bunny chocolates Biggy Piggy boxed;
If Biggy Piggy boxed a box of bunny chocolates,
Then where's the box of bunny chocolates Biggy Piggy boxed?

Little Miss Muffet

Little Miss Muffet sat on a tuffet,
Eating of curds and whey;
There came a big spider, and sat down beside her,
And frightened Miss Muffet away.

Lilly McMuffin

Lilly McMuffin sat by her oven,
To see when her muffins were done.
She left for a minute, her brother got in it,
And Lilly McMuffin got none.

Little Boy Blue

Little Boy Blue, come, blow your horn!
The sheep's in the meadow, the cow's in the corn.
Where's the little boy that looks after the sheep?
Under the haystack, fast asleep!

A Calf Named Moo

A calf named Moo was born in a barn.
He didn't like being down on the farm.
He longed to be a computer geek.
So he left his family his fortune to seek.

Humpty Dumpty

Humpty Dumpty sat on a wall,
Humpty Dumpty had a great fall;
All the King's horses and all the King's men
Cannot put Humpty together again.

Morty Frompney

Morty Frompney always had a ball.
His only problem: he was so tall.
He didn't duck, so he bumped his head,
Got a headache and went to bed.

Old King Cole

Old King Cole
Was a merry old soul,
And a merry old soul was he;

He called for his pipe,
And he called for his bowl,
And he called for his fiddlers three!

And every fiddler; he had a fine fiddle,
And a very fine fiddle had he.
"Twee tweedle dee, tweedle dee," went the fiddlers.

Oh, there's none so rare,
As can compare,
With King Cole and his fiddlers three.

Old Mole Joel

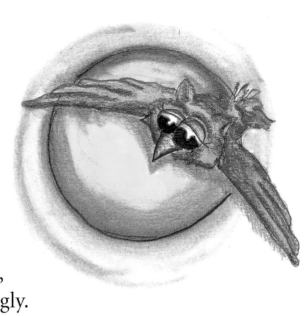

Old Mole Joel
Lived in a hole.
He lived quite happily.

He lived with his wife,
And he lived with his son,
And a daughter who was giggly.

Each night he went out,
But went carefully.

Because old mister Owl
Was on the prowl,
To eat any mole he could see.

Pat-A-Cake

Pat-a-cake, pat-a-cake,
Baker's man!
So I do, master,
As fast as I can.

Pat it, and prick it,
And mark it with T,
Put it in the oven
For Tommy and me.

Pinky Pig

Pinky Pig, Pinky Pig
Come on by.
Come very quickly
So baby won't cry.
Snort her and roll her,
And play with her please.
Then we'll eat a dinner
Of corn mixed with cheese.

This Little Pig Went to Market

This little pig went to market;
This little pig stayed at home;
This little pig had roast beef;
This little pig had none;
This little pig cried, "Wee, wee, wee!"
All the way home.

This Little Kitty

'Alley Cat' kitty went to New York.
'Home Body' kitty stayed home.
'High Class' kitty to London,
'Adventure' kitty to Rome.
Momma kitty cried,
"Meow, Meow, Meow,"
And all the kitties came home.

Now you try it! *Try to do a "Mother Goose, Other Goose" for yourself.*

1. Take an 8 ½ x 11 piece of paper and fold it in half.

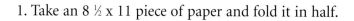

fold here

8 ½"

11"

2. On one half write a "Mother Goose" rhyme and draw a picture for it.

3. On the other half write an "Other Goose" rhyme and draw a picture to go with it.

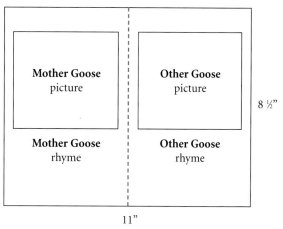

Mother Goose
picture

Other Goose
picture

Mother Goose
rhyme

Other Goose
rhyme

8 ½"

11"

For more information on how to do this and to enter VanitaBooks "Mother Goose, Other Goose" contest, go to our website: www.VanitaBooks.com

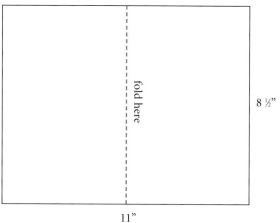

The Art

To create an old fashioned nostalgic feel, the illustrations for *Mother Goose, Other Goose* were sketched and shaded in #2 Graphite pencil on Canson 90 lb Watercolor paper. Bright colors of Gouache were added to liven up the "Other Goose" illustration with splashes of color spilling over into the traditional "Mother Goose" illustration. The finished art was sprayed with a matte sealer to prevent the graphite from smudging. The artwork was scanned and the images were placed in the layout to create *Mother Goose, Other Goose*.

Vanita Oelschlager

Vanita Oelschlager is a wife, mother, grandmother, former teacher, caregiver, author, and poet. She was named "Writer in Residence" for the Literacy Program at The University of Akron in 2007. She is a graduate of Mount Union College, where she is currently a member of the Board of Trustees. She wants to encourage children to write and illustrate their own *Mother Goose, Other Goose* rhymes.

Robin Hegan

Robin Hegan doesn't consider herself an illustrator, rather a small town girl who has a passion to share her imagination with others through her drawings. Robin grew up in the Laurel Mountains of Pennsylvania where imagination took her and her childhood friends on many adventures. After graduating from Pennsylvania State University with a degree in Integrative Arts, Robin resided in Ohio for several years until she and her husband Matt decided to return to that small town in Pennsylvania to raise their two girls, Kendall and Kya. In addition to *Mother Goose, Other Goose*, Robin's illustrations can also be seen in *My Grampy Can't Walk* and *The Lizard House Adventure*.